P9-CMN-467

PLEASE WASH
YOUR HANDS
BEFORE YOU READ ME
AND KEEP ME CLEAN

THE BOYS

By Jeff Newman

Simon & Schuster Books for Young Readers
New York London Toronto Sydney

For Dad, and in memory of Frank

SIMON & SCHUSTER BOOKS FOR YOUNG READERS
An imprint of Simon & Schuster Children's Publishing Division
1230 Avenue of the Americas, New York, New York 10020

Book design by Lucy Ruth Cummins
The text for this book is set in Bullion.
The illustrations for this book are rendered in gouache and ink.
Manufactured in China
10 9 8 7 6 5 4 3 2 1
Library of Congress Cataloging-in-Publication Data
Newman, Jeff, 1976-
The boys / written by Jeff Newman ; illustrated by
Jeff Newman.—1st ed.
p. cm.
Summary: A shy boy, seeking the courage to play baseball
with the other children in a park, is coaxed out of his shell by
some "old timers" sitting nearby who, in turn, discover they are
still in the game.
ISBN: 978-1-4169-5012-7 (hardcover : alk. paper)
[1. Bashfulness—Fiction. 2. Baseball—Fiction. 3. Old age—
Fiction. 4. Stories without words.] I. Title.
PZ7.N47984Boy 2010
[E]—dc22
2007047985

TUESDAY

WEDNESDAY

THURSDAY

FRIDAY

SATURDAY

SUNDAY

MONDAY

TUESDAY